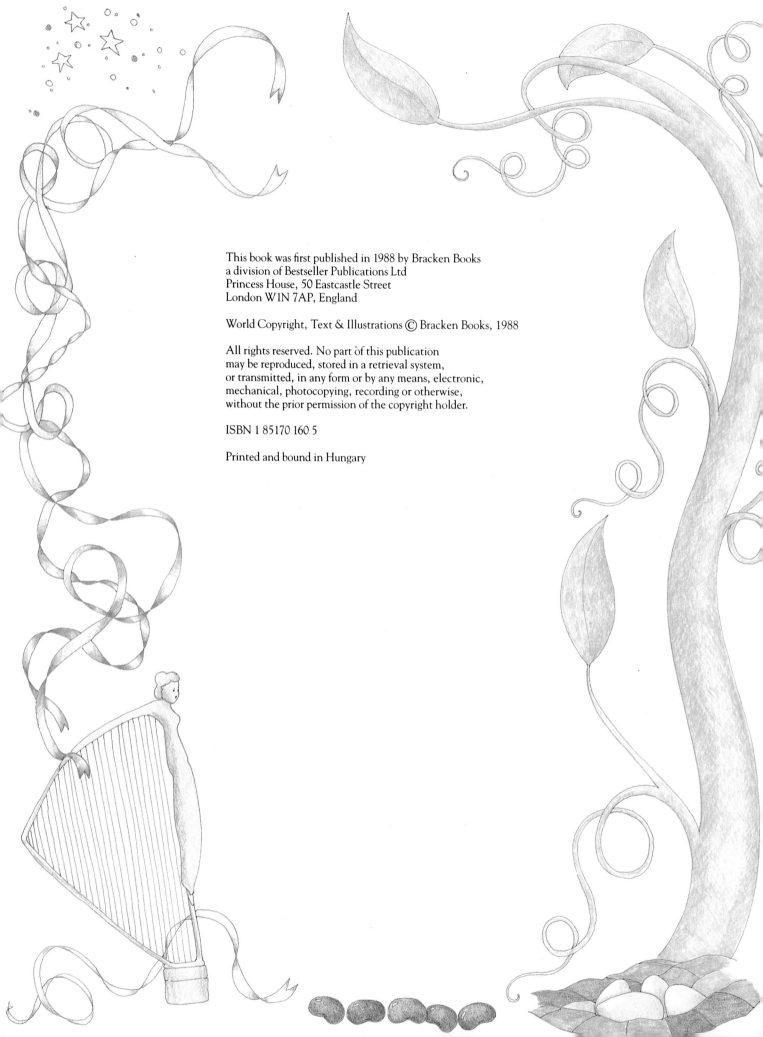

This book was first published in 1988 by Bracken Books
a division of Bestseller Publications Ltd
Princess House, 50 Eastcastle Street
London W1N 7AP, England

ISBN 1 85170 160 5

Printed and bound in Hungary

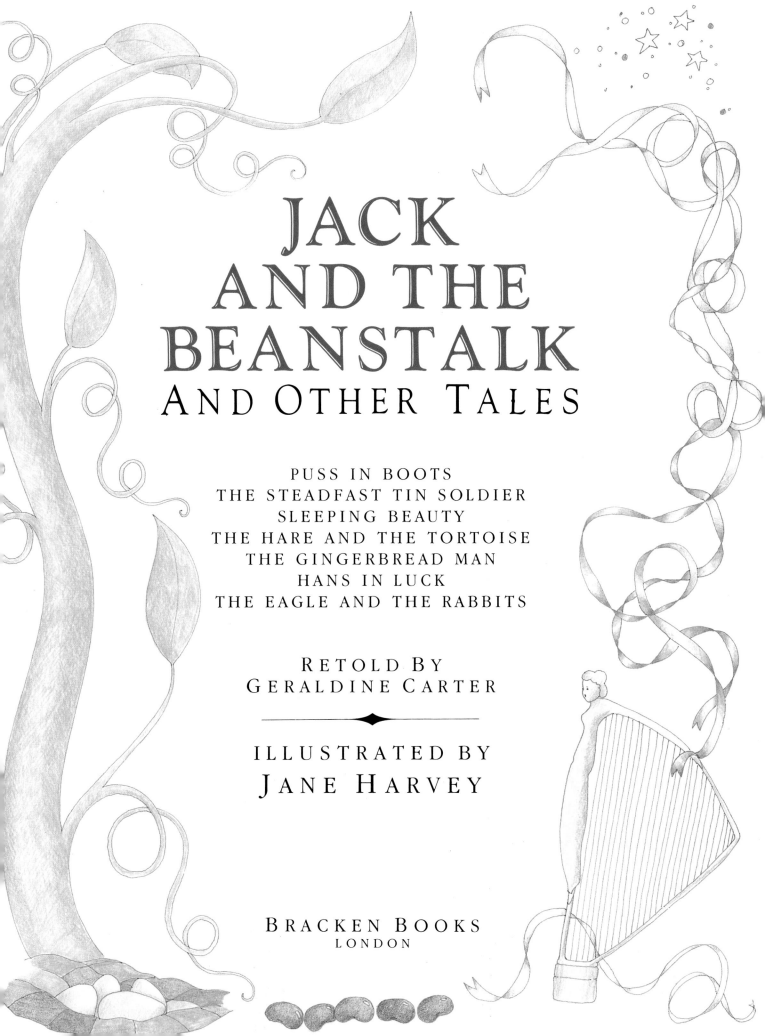

Jack and the Beanstalk
And Other Tales

PUSS IN BOOTS
THE STEADFAST TIN SOLDIER
SLEEPING BEAUTY
THE HARE AND THE TORTOISE
THE GINGERBREAD MAN
HANS IN LUCK
THE EAGLE AND THE RABBITS

RETOLD BY
GERALDINE CARTER

ILLUSTRATED BY
JANE HARVEY

BRACKEN BOOKS
LONDON

Jack and the Beanstalk

In a small cottage, once upon a time, there lived an old widow with her son, Jack. Now Jack was a heedless, lazy lad who never bothered with work. Instead, he sold off his mother's possessions one by one until all she had left was her dear cow, Milky White.

One day Jack burst into the house calling: "Mother, where's my cake?" "Oh, you selfish, greedy boy, Jack!" she scolded. "Have you no thought for me? Day after day I toil for you, and now you have sold almost everything I own. There is not a scrap of bread left to eat, and certainly no cake. We shall starve, thanks to you!"

"Don't fuss so, Mother," Jack retorted, "we've still got the old cow, haven't we? I'll go to the market today and sell her." "Certainly not!" cried his mother indignantly, "I forbid you to take her away. For ten years she has given me fresh milk, which is more than can be said for you!" But Jack nagged, and pleaded, and bullied, and coaxed until his mother finally gave in. And off he hurried to market before she could change her mind.

As Jack was strutting along the road leading the cow to market, he met an old pedlar. "Good-day, my fine fellow!" said the cheerful pedlar "and where are you going with that old cow?" "Don't call this an old cow!" said Jack. "She's not very old, and I'm hoping to get a good price for her at market." "A good price for *that* ancient thing!" snorted the crafty pedlar, "you won't get much for her. If you like, I'll let you have all these marvelous beans in exchange for your scraggy creature. Just take a close look at them!"

The pedlar held out his hat and Jack peered at the multitude of shiny, brightly colored beans. What a sight! Of course he readily agreed to the bargain. And so the gleeful pedlar hobbled off with the cow as Jack rushed home with the beans. "Look what I've got," he called, proudly displaying his beans. "What?" screamed the poor widow. "Do you mean to tell me that you have swopped my precious Milky White for a paltry handful of *beans*. How could you do such a thing? And seizing the beans, she hurled them straight out of the window.

Early next morning when Jack awoke, he was puzzled, for he could not see clearly out of his window. Into the garden he hurried and what did he find but a huge, great beanstalk, so tall that its top was lost in the clouds. His beans had sprouted during the night and already thick, green stalks had twined together, forming a kind of ladder. He decided at once to climb the beanstalk and seek his fortune.

Up and up Jack climbed, higher and higher until, passing through drifting, icy clouds, he reached the top. Here he found himself in a barren desert; not a single bird or animal was to be seen, not a tree, not even a shrub. Jack walked northwards, hoping to find some sign of life. But he did not see a single building until sunset, when, at last, he caught sight of a large, ugly mansion. He stumbled towards the building as fast as his weary legs could carry him and pounded on the door. A thin, tall woman answered his knock.

"A human!" she gasped on seeing Jack. "Foolish boy! Run, run, as fast as you can! Get away from here, quickly! My husband is a giant and if he finds you here then he'll gobble you up before you can say *boo!* Boys on toast – his favourite meal. Oh dear me! Why ever did you come here?" "*Please* can you give me some food and let me rest awhile," Jack begged. "I'm far too tired to run anywhere, and I will drop dead of hunger before I go two strides further."

"Oh . . . poor boy!" said the woman sympathetically. "Come in then, just for a little while. But don't say I didn't warn you!" She produced, for Jack, a large loaf of bread and a jug of milk. He munched away happily, until he heard a sudden thumping and banging noise from the door which shook the whole house.

"Mercy on us!" cried the horrified woman, turning white as death, "it's the giant! Whatever shall I do? When he finds you here, he'll kill me for disobeying him and then he'll grill you alive. Oh dear, oh dear me! Quick! I'll hide you in the oven." So she bundled the boy into the

oven and there he crouched, trembling like a leaf.

Jack listened in terror as the giant strode round and round the kitchen, sniffing suspiciously. Suddenly his deep voice boomed out:

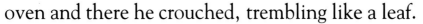

"Fee-fi-fo-fum, I smell the blood of an Englishman!
Be he alive or be he dead, I'll grind his bones to make my bread!"

Jack froze with horror but the giant's wife protested: "Why, husband, there are no Englishmen here, indeed not! How could you think that? Don't you know I'd never let anyone into the house when you are out, let alone an *Englishman?* Your keen nose must have sniffed at that lump of raw meat the crows brought in."

"Alright, alright!" snarled the bad-tempered giant, "stop going on about it; we all make mistakes, don't we? Just get on and fetch me my supper." The woman scurried to do his bidding and for more than an hour the giant sat stuffing himself at the table.

Poor Jack crouched, terribly cramped, in the oven. When, at last, the giant finished his enormous meal he roared: "Bring me my hen!"

Peeping through a crack in the oven door, Jack saw the giant for the first time: a huge, mean-looking man with squinty little eyes and a great bulbous nose. Not long after, his wife appeared, a large brown hen tucked under one arm. She quickly put it on the table and hurried away.

"Lay!" commanded the giant, glaring at the hen. No sooner had he uttered the words than the hen clucked a couple of loud "cluck-clucks" and produced a gleaming, solid gold egg. "Lay!" he repeated and, sure enough, the hen laid another egg, even larger than the last. This continued for ages, until the table was quite littered with golden eggs. Finally the giant got tired, leaned back in his chair, yawned and fell asleep.

Jack was not slow to take his chance. He crept out of the oven and tip-toed up to the table. Then he grabbed hold of the hen, rushed out of the house and ran back to the beanstalk as fast as his legs would carry him.

Down the beanstalk he scrambled, clutching the hen tightly. At last, he arrived back in his very own garden.

Jack hurried indoors, eager to tell his mother about his adventures. But there she was at the kitchen table, crying bitterly, certain that he had come to some grisly end. "Now, now, Mother," said Jack impatiently, "stop crying, at once, and have a look at this hen. Isn't she wonderful?" "Er – if you say so," replied his Mother, glancing doubtfully at the hen. "But, Jack, it will take more than one hen to prevent us from starving, you know. Does it lay good eggs, I wonder?"

"Lay good eggs!" cried Jack. "I should jolly well think it does. *Lay!*" he ordered and, a second later, there was a fine golden egg rolling about on the table. "You see how clever I am, Mother!" said Jack gleefully. "Thanks to me, now we'll have stacks of golden eggs, millions of them. I got a good bargain for the old cow, you must admit." "Oh, I do admit it," said the widow. "You are *such* a clever boy, Jack. But then, I always knew it."

For months Jack and his Mother sold golden eggs but gradually Jack became bored: "What other treasures has the old giant got up that beanstalk, I wonder?" he thought.

One morning, after breakfast, Jack rose suddenly and called out: "See you later, Mother. I'm just going for a little trip up the beanstalk." Jack's mother wept and implored him not to go, but bold Jack took not the slightest notice. Off he went, and up and up the beanstalk he climbed. When he reached the top, Jack ran all the way to the giant's mansion, and nervously knocked at the door. The giant's wife answered. "Good grief! Another human!" she cried, "if I were you, my boy, I would dash off as fast as my legs could carry me. Know you not that my husband is the most ferocious giant in the land? Nothing delights him more than a freshly-cooked slice of boy." "*I'm* not afraid of giants!" boasted Jack untruthfully. "So can you let me in for a moment? I'm boiling out here – surely you can spare a glass of water?"

"Better to boil in the sun than boil in the saucepan!" replied the giant's wife. "I wouldn't dare let another boy into the house. Some young brat stole my husband's precious hen. I've never heard the last of that. Wait a moment, though," she added, staring at Jack, "don't I know you? Aren't *you* the wretch that ran off with the hen?"

"Certainly not!" cried Jack in alarm, "I've never seen you before in my life! What's this hen you keep going on about?"

"Never you mind!" she said, "you can come in then, just for a little. But if my husband comes back, watch out!"

The giant's wife gave Jack food and drink but as he was eating there came a loud knock-knocking on the door. Quick as a flash, Jack dived across the room into the oven. The giant's wife slammed the oven door behind him, and hurried to let in her husband. "Er – hello, dear," she said nervously, "did you have a nice day?"

"*Have a nice day?*" repeated the giant. "What's that supposed to mean? I haven't had a nice day for months now. There's not a boy to be smelt for miles." Abruptly he stopped talking and stood still, giving a couple of bloodcurdling sniffs. "But what's this now?" and he roared:

"Fe-fi-fo-fum, I smell the blood of an Englishman!
Be he alive or be he dead, I'll grind his bones to make my bread!"

Jack shivered with fear. "Why, oh *why* did I come here again?" he moaned to himself in terror, "once should have been enough to warn me. Blow the beanstalk!" But at that moment the giant's wife butted in: "Stuff and nonsense!" she snapped bravely. "Englishman, twiddle-twaddle! You've got Englishmen on the brain, that's all. There's nothing to smell but the roast lamb for supper."

So the giant sat down at table, and wolfed down a great saddle of lamb. Jack, crammed in the oven, was growing more uncomfortable by the minute. But, at last, the giant grew tired of eating and called for his moneybags. Peering through a crack, Jack saw the long-suffering wife lugging leather bags into the kitchen. The giant opened them and tipped them, one by one, right over the table. Gold and silver rolled around and the giant chuckled in delight. Poor Jack turned green with envy.

Later, the giant swept away the coins into their bags, and called for his harp. "Play," he shouted, and the harp played wonderful music. Soon the giant was soothed to sleep and Jack slipped from the oven. He reached out, seized the harp with one hand and, with the other, grabbed a moneybag. Jack wasted not a second; he dashed from the house and ran as hard as he could back towards the beanstalk. But the harp was enchanted. "Master! Master!" it cried, "a rascal runs with me! Help Me! Help!"

The giant stirred and awoke. Instantly he set off in pursuit, striding furiously after Jack, roaring out insults. At last Jack reached the beanstalk with the giant hot on his heels. Jack dropped the moneybag, down, down, and scrambled after it, still clinging tightly to the harp. He reached the bottom and found his Mother scurrying about the garden, snatching up coins. "Quick, Mother!" Jack screamed, "out of the way," and as he grabbed an axe lying by the door there appeared, through the cloud-covered top of the beanstalk, first one huge foot, then a second. The beanstalk shook and swayed. Jack swung hard at its base with his axe – once, twice, three times. It creaked, it groaned, and with a great CRASH, down it fell. The giant tumbled headlong to the ground and there lay dead.

Jack and his mother hugged each other for joy and Jack heartily begged pardon for his disobedience. And so they lived happily together for many long years, and Jack was as faithful a son as any mother could wish for.

Puss in Boots

Once upon a time there lived an old miller with three sons. He was so poor that all he had in the world was a mill, a donkey and a cat. When the miller died his eldest son took the mill, the second son was given the donkey, and the youngest son was left with the cat. "Well I never," cried the youngest son in astonishment, "is this all I'm to be given? Once I've killed this young creature and sold its fur to make a hat, then I'll be left with nothing at all. Nothing!"

The cat curled up by the fire and listened intently to his master: "Kill me?" he interrupted at last, "indeed, I hope not! You should know better than that, Master. Now if you do as I say, I shall make your

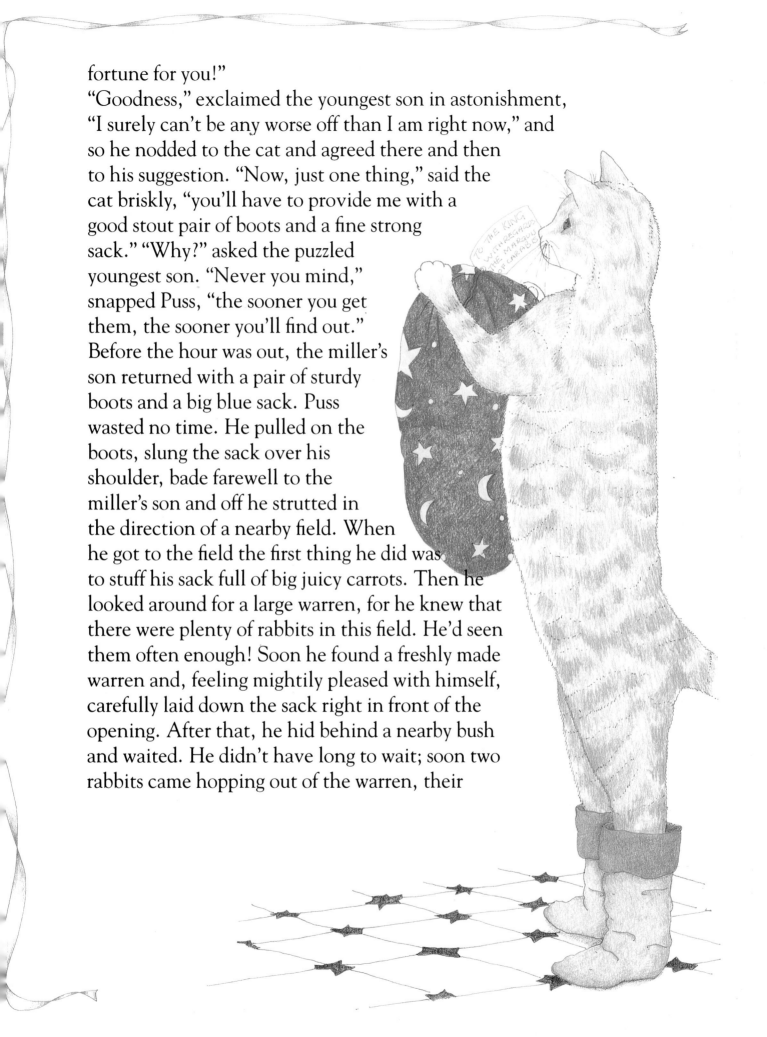

fortune for you!"

"Goodness," exclaimed the youngest son in astonishment, "I surely can't be any worse off than I am right now," and so he nodded to the cat and agreed there and then to his suggestion. "Now, just one thing," said the cat briskly, "you'll have to provide me with a good stout pair of boots and a fine strong sack." "Why?" asked the puzzled youngest son. "Never you mind," snapped Puss, "the sooner you get them, the sooner you'll find out." Before the hour was out, the miller's son returned with a pair of sturdy boots and a big blue sack. Puss wasted no time. He pulled on the boots, slung the sack over his shoulder, bade farewell to the miller's son and off he strutted in the direction of a nearby field. When he got to the field the first thing he did was to stuff his sack full of big juicy carrots. Then he looked around for a large warren, for he knew that there were plenty of rabbits in this field. He'd seen them often enough! Soon he found a freshly made warren and, feeling mightily pleased with himself, carefully laid down the sack right in front of the opening. After that, he hid behind a nearby bush and waited. He didn't have long to wait; soon two rabbits came hopping out of the warren, their noses twitching as they smelt the freshly pulled carrots. Right into the sack they jumped for a little nibble and, quick as a flash, Puss leapt from behind the tree and pulled the string of the sack as tight as can be.

Well satisfied with his cunning, Puss slung the sack over his shoulder and marched straight off to the palace. When he reached the gates of the palace itself he demanded to see no less a person than the king.

As Puss was shown into the Council Chamber he bowed low before the king: "Good day, Your Majesty!" he cried, "my master, the Marquis of Carabas" (for this was the name he decided to give his master) "has asked me to present Your Majesty with this splendid pair of juicy rabbits!" and so he handed the sack to the king who opened it and nodded in delight: "Capital, capital," he said, and thanked the cat warmly. "Tell your master I am most touched by his gift." A day or two later, Puss presented the king with two plump partridges he had managed to snare in a cornfield and over the next few months Puss returned again and again to the palace, each time bearing gifts for the king.

One day, the cat discovered that the king and his only daughter planned to take a ride along by the banks of the river. In a great state of excitement he rushed back to the miller's son: "Master, master, come down with me to the river at once. Your fortune is made!"

Well, the miller's son could hardly believe his ears. How could he refuse such a splendid offer! Off they both charged to the river, as fast as their legs would carry them. When they got to the water's edge, Puss ordered his master to take off his clothes and to jump straight into the river. How cold and muddy it seemed, but as the miller's son shook the water from his eyes he saw the King's golden coach rolling into view. The next thing that caught his eye was Puss, dashing towards the coach, screeching at the top of his voice:

"Help! Help! The Marquis of Carabas is drowning! Save him, I beg you, save him!"

Now, on hearing this sad plea for help, the king immediately ordered his guards to rescue the kind marquis, who, after all, had been the source of all his splendid gifts. Just as the king's guards were pulling the miller's son out from the muddy water, Puss ran up to the carriage once more. He was looking most distressed and breathlessly panted out his sad story:

"Terrible tragedy! While my master was bathing, some thieves crept up to the bank and stole his clothes! Alas, the Marquis of Carabas has nothing left to wear!" But, of course, it was the artful cat himself who had hidden his master's worn-out clothes beneath a large stone. Yet the king had no reason to doubt the kind cat's words and so he ordered two guards to race back to the palace and to fetch one of his very best robes for the marquis.

Dressed, at last, in the king's splendid robes, the miller's son looked really quite grand. Even Puss was surprised. In fact, he looked so splendid that the king's daughter was mightily impressed and she invited him at once to join the royal party.

The cat did not linger but hurried on ahead of the royal party and soon came to a large field full of harvest workers. "The king is coming," he announced, "if he should ask who owns this field, tell him that it belongs to the great and noble Marquis of Carabas."

Then Puss arched his back, flattened his ears, puffed himself up and hissed as hard as he could: "If anyone disobeys me, you'll all be chopped into mincemeat, chopped into tiny portions of mincemeat, all of you," and off he stalked still looking as fierce as could be. Just a few moments later, the king riding along in his coach saw the harvesters hard at work. Poking his head out of the window, His Majesty asked them who it was who owned the vast fields in which they worked. "They belong to the great and noble Marquis of Carabas," answered the harvesters without hesitation, for the cat's threats had filled them with great fear. The king, much impressed, drove on. Ahead of him the crafty cat scampered, ordering everyone he met to tell the king that all the lands, as far as the eye could see, belonged to the brave and powerful Marquis of Carabas.

Eventually the cat arrived at a great house, where dwelt a fearsome ogre, the richest ever known; for all the lands which

the king and the cat had passed through really belonged to this
fellow. The cat, full of confidence after his cunning day's work,
boldly marched through the gates and into the great hall, where the
ogre himself was seated. Bowing low he said: "My lord ogre, what an
honour it is for me to see you! I have heard it said that you have the
power to transform yourself into any kind of bird or beast living upon
this earth. For many years I have longed to ask you if this is true."
"Of course it's true" snarled the ogre, "and to prove it to you, I'll turn
myself into a lion!" In a second he had carried out his threat, and the
huge, roaring lion standing before him so terrified poor Puss that
with great difficulty – owing to his boots – he leapt up onto a
cupboard. "Ha ha ha!" roared the ogre, "that gave you a fright, didn't
it, my friend?" The cat admitted that the lion had indeed given him
quite a fright. "But how much more skill would be needed for your
lordship to turn himself into something small, a mouse for instance,"
said the cat breathlessly. "Only a really *clever* ogre could do that," he
added. "I *am* a really clever ogre!" boomed the ogre, "and just to
prove it, I shall turn myself into a mouse!"

And the foolish ogre *did* turn himself into a mouse, whereupon Puss pounced upon him, quick as a flash, and gobbled him all up. Meanwhile the King, driving through the countryside in his coach, saw the fine house and decided he should honour it with his presence. Puss, who heard the sound of the coach wheels clattering, rushed out to greet the king. "Welcome, Your Majesty, to the home of the Marquis of Carabas!" he said, bowing lower than ever. "Well, well, well!" cried the king, quite flabbergasted. "This splendid house is yours too, Marquis? You must be the richest man in my kingdom! I can't think of anyone I would rather have as my son-in-law. Would you, by any chance, care to marry my daughter?"

The miller's son was delighted to accept the honour and within a week he and the princess were married and settled happily into the ogre's house. And, as for Puss, he became a great lord and never again was known to chase another mouse, except in the way of sport.

The Steadfast Tin Soldier

Once upon a time there were five and twenty tin soldiers, all brothers, all made from the same tin spoon. The very first sounds they heard, as the lid was lifted from their box, were those of a little boy crying: "Soldiers, soldiers!" as he clapped his hands in delight. It was the boy's birthday and the soldiers were his special present. One by one, he picked them out of the box and arranged them on the table. There they were, each one in his smart red and blue uniform, shouldering his gun and looking straight ahead. They all looked the same, except for one, for he had but one leg. That soldier had been the very last to be made from the spoon and there was too little tin to finish him. But, on his one leg, he stood just as well as the others did on their two and, in fact, our story is all about him.

On the table there were many other toys, the most beautiful of all a paper castle. You could see through its tiny windows, right into the castle rooms. Outside the castle little trees surrounded a small mirror lake whose surface reflected the wax swans swimming about on it. At the entrance to this castle there stood a little maiden. She, too, was cut from paper, but she was wearing a dress of the lightest gauze, with a little blue ribbon, like a scarf, draped over her shoulders. Pinned to the scarf was a brilliant spangle, almost as large as her whole face. The little girl stood there with her arms outstretched, for she was a dancer. One of her legs was raised so high in the air the tin soldier could not see it. He thought that she, like himself, only had one leg.

"What a perfect wife she would make but she is much too grand for

me. She lives in a castle and I only live in a box and even that I share with my brothers. No, that certainly will not do." But he wanted to get to know her and so he stationed himself behind a snuff box and watched as she stood there on one leg and never lost her balance.

In the evening, after the other soldiers had been packed away into the box, and everyone in the house had gone to sleep, the rest of the toys started to play. They danced, and they fought battles; the nutcrackers turned somersaults, and even the pencil scribbled away on the slate. In fact, they made such a noise they even woke up the canary and he instantly joined in the merriment. The poor tin soldiers wanted to play too, and so they rustled about in their box trying as hard as they could to shake off its lid, but nothing would shift it. Only two toys in the room remained quiet, unmoving; the little dancer and the tin soldier. She stood, as stiff as ever, on tip-toe, her arms outstretched and he, behind the snuff box, did not take his eyes off her for a single moment.

At last the clock struck twelve and – *pop* – up flew the lid of the snuff box. There was no snuff in it, no; instead, a little black goblin, a sort of Jack-in-the-box. A

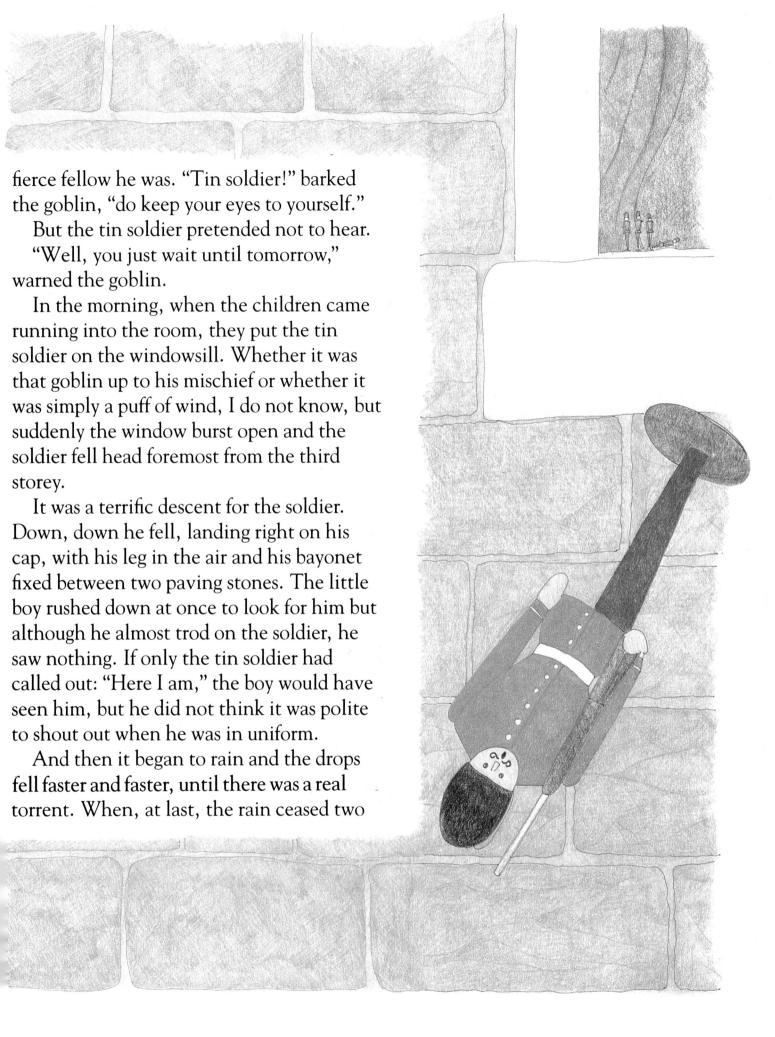

fierce fellow he was. "Tin soldier!" barked the goblin, "do keep your eyes to yourself."

But the tin soldier pretended not to hear.

"Well, you just wait until tomorrow," warned the goblin.

In the morning, when the children came running into the room, they put the tin soldier on the windowsill. Whether it was that goblin up to his mischief or whether it was simply a puff of wind, I do not know, but suddenly the window burst open and the soldier fell head foremost from the third storey.

It was a terrific descent for the soldier. Down, down he fell, landing right on his cap, with his leg in the air and his bayonet fixed between two paving stones. The little boy rushed down at once to look for him but although he almost trod on the soldier, he saw nothing. If only the tin soldier had called out: "Here I am," the boy would have seen him, but he did not think it was polite to shout out when he was in uniform.

And then it began to rain and the drops fell faster and faster, until there was a real torrent. When, at last, the rain ceased two

boys came walking along the street and stopped right in front of the house. "Mind out!" said one, "look, there's a tin soldier. Come on, let's have some fun. Let's make him go for a sail."

So they made a boat out of newspaper and placed the soldier right in the middle of it. Then they gave the boat a push and the soldier was swept along in the gutter, with the boys running alongside clapping their hands and shouting with glee. The paper boat bobbed up and down, and from time to time it whirled round and round. The tin soldier felt alarmed and quite giddy but he never moved a muscle; he just looked straight ahead with his gun shouldered. And then, as the boat drifted under a long wooden tunnel, dark as the inside of the soldiers' packing box, he thought: "What on earth am I going to do? It must surely all be the fault of that goblin! Oh, if only the little maiden were with me in the boat, I wouldn't care about the dark."

At that moment, a big water rat from the tunnel approached him. "Have you a pass?" asked the rat. "Come on, hand up your pass!"

The tin soldier did not speak; instead he clung still tighter to his gun. The boat rushed on, the rat close behind. Phew, how that rat gnashed his teeth and shouted at the sticks and straws: "Stop him, stop him, he hasn't paid his money, he hasn't shown his pass!"

But the current grew stronger and stronger and now, at last, the tin soldier could see daylight at the end of the tunnel. He was also aware of a roaring sound, the sort of sound which would strike terror into the heart of the bravest soldier. Just imagine! At the end of that tunnel his stream rushed straight into a huge canal.

The soldier was so near to the end of the tunnel he could not stop. The boat swept on and on, out into the canal and the poor tin soldier held himself as stiff as can be. No one might say of him that he was afraid.

Three or four times the boat swirled round, filling with water right up to its edge. It was going to sink. The tin soldier stood up to his neck in the water and watched as the boat sank deeper and deeper. The paper became more limp, and soon the water covered his head. All of a sudden he thought of the pretty little dancer whom he might never see again, and that thought gave him a new strength. But then the paper gave way completely and the soldier fell through the bottom – straight into the mouth of a big fish.

Oh how dark it

seemed inside the fish, darker than the tunnel, and so cramped. But the tin soldier, steadfast as ever, lay there full length, shouldering his gun.

The fish thrashed about making frantic movements but after some time it became quiet. Much later, the soldier saw a flash like lightning. Someone had pierced the fish with a knife for that fish had been caught, taken to market, sold and brought to the kitchen. And there was the cook standing over it, cutting it open with a large kitchen knife. "A tin soldier!" she exclaimed as she bent over the fish. Then she picked him up carefully between two fingers and carried him into the parlour.

Everyone was curious to see the wonderful soldier who had travelled about in the stomach of a fish, but the tin solder didn't feel in the slightest bit proud. After a while he was lifted up again and carried to a table and, do you know, he found himself in the very same room, with the same children, and the same toys still standing on the table. There, too, stood the beautiful castle and the lovely dancer.

The dancer was still standing on one leg, holding the other up in the

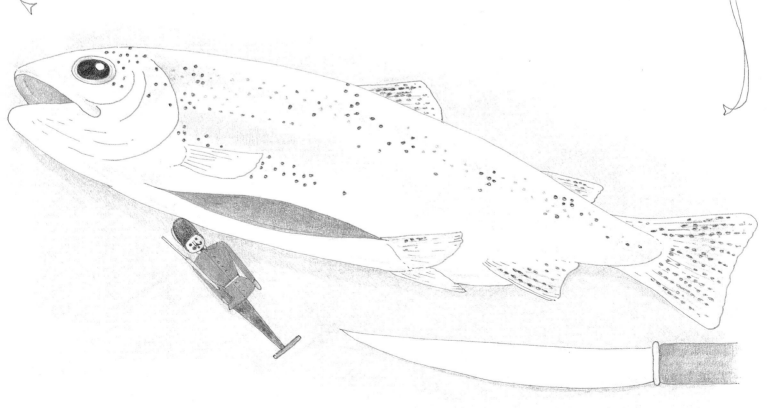

air. You see, she also was unbending. The soldier was so touched he was ready to shed tears of tin, but that would have been unfitting for a soldier. He looked at the dancer and she looked at him but they said never a word. At that moment one of the little boys grabbed the tin soldier and without rhyme or reason threw him into the fire. No doubt the little goblin in the snuff box was to blame.

The tin soldier stood there in the middle of the most intense heat, lit up by the flame; but whether it was the heat of the fire, or the warmth of his feelings, he did not know. All his bright color had gone; it might have vanished during his perilous journey, or it might have vanished through grief, who can tell? He looked at the little maiden and she looked at him and he felt that he was melting away, but still he managed to keep himself erect, bravely shouldering his gun.

A door opened, the draught caught hold of the little dancer who fluttered like a sylph straight into the fire, to the soldier. The fire blazed around her and she was gone!

By this time the soldier was reduced to a mere lump, but when the maid took away the ashes next morning she found him there in the shape of a small tin heart. All that was left of the dancer was her spangle, and that was burnt as black as coal.

Sleeping Beauty

Once upon a time, in a far-off kingdom, there lived a king and queen who for many years longed for a child. At last, when they had almost given up hope, the queen gave birth to a healthy daughter. Everywhere in the land the king's subjects rejoiced and great preparations were made for the christening of the new princess.

Seven fairies were invited to act as godparents to the newborn child, and when the christening was over the king held a magnificent banquet in their honour. Set before each fairy was a gleaming golden plate, and a golden knife, fork, and spoon, sparkling with diamonds and rubies. But as the guests took their places at table, into the great hall there hobbled an old hunchbacked fairy. She was as ugly as can be, and the king and queen gasped in dismay, for this was old Mistress Stickleback. She had lived alone in a tall, distant tower for so long everyone had forgotten her.

"Well!" snarled the evil old fairy, "here's a fine welcome! You didn't expect me to come to your daughter's christening, I'm sure. What a pleasant surprise this must be for everyone!"

Hastily, the king ordered his servants to set another place at table, but there was no golden plate for the fairy, for only seven had been made.

At once Mistress Stickleback started to complain: "Where is *my* golden plate, where is my knife and fork?" she demanded. "How dare you insult me like this!" She was outraged and would listen to no-one, but sat there muttering threats beneath her breath.

At last the meal was ended, and the fairies were ushered into the room where the princess lay asleep in her cradle. Now each was to bestow something special upon the child, and one by one they announced their gifts. The first fairy let it be known that the princess would be blessed with great beauty; the second, that she would be famous for her wisdom; the third, that she would move with grace; the fourth promised her a voice like a lark; the fifth, that she would play all musical instruments perfectly; and the sixth, that she would always enjoy excellent health. As the seventh fairy opened her mouth, old Fairy Stickleback shoved her out of the way and hobbled up to the cradle. She was trembling from top to toe with rage.

"My turn to give a gift now!" she cried. "The child can live until she is sixteen but

after that time she will prick her finger on a spindle and die! What good will the gift of beauty and other gifts be to her when she is dead?" The fairy unleashed an unholy cackle of glee, spun round and disappeared.

The whole palace was in turmoil but suddenly the seventh fairy stepped forward and called: "Wait! I have not yet given my gift! Alas, I am not powerful enough to undo the bad fairy's spell but I can change it. The princess will not die by pricking her finger. She will only sleep, but she will sleep deeply for one hundred years and then she will be awakened by the kiss of a handsome prince."

No, this could not happen; this terrible accident must be prevented! And so, in order to ensure that no spindle ever pricked the finger of their precious daughter the king and queen ordered that, on pain of death, every single spindle in their kingdom should be destroyed.

A few days after her sixteenth birthday, the princess went exploring in one of the old, deserted towers of the palace. Hurrying through the cobweb-filled, dust-covered rooms, she came unexpectedly upon a little old woman who was sitting, busily spinning.

"Oh hello!" said the princess, much surprised that

anyone should live there. "What on earth are you doing?"

Now this old woman had lived in the dusty tower of the palace for so many years that everyone had forgotten all about her. She had never been told that spindles were not allowed in the land, and she was astonished at the girl's ignorance. "Why, I'm spinning, of course," she answered sharply. "Anyone could see that. Don't say that you don't know how to spin! Why, when I was your age I was already famous for my spinning. Tut, tut, tut! Sit down at once, child, and I'll teach you how to spin since no one else has bothered to do so."

The princess eagerly grasped the spindle and began to follow the old woman's instructions, until, all of a sudden, the spindle slipped in her hand and pierced her finger. "Ow!"

shrieked the princess as she fell heavily to the ground.

The old woman, not knowing what to do, cried out for help. Soon half the court was crowding round the princess, trying to awaken her. They shook her, they drenched her with water, they unlaced the back of her dress; they even slapped her. But all their efforts were in vain, and the beautiful princess lay still as death on the floor.

By this time the king and queen had appeared, and at once they realised that the princess had pricked her finger. The bad fairy's spell had come true in spite of all their efforts. The king immediately sent one of his servants to summon the good fairy. While the sorrowing king and queen and their courtiers waited for her to come, they gently lifted up the sleeping princess, carried her up the main stairway, and placed her on the best bed in the palace.

After what seemed like a very long time, the good fairy arrived and greeted the distressed king and queen. But she shook her head, saying: "There is nothing that I can do to break the spell before the hundred years are over, alas. But when the princess does awaken I do not want her to be lonely and so I shall send every single person in this castle, and all the animals living here, into a deep slumber."

Without further ado, the good fairy waved her wand and muttered her spell. And instantly everyone, from the king and queen, right down to the smallest page-boy and the greasiest skullery

maid, toppled to one side and fell asleep. The animals, too, stirred no more.

The next hundred years passed slowly by. A dark, dense, thorny forest grew up around the castle, forming a barrier through which no man or beast could pass. Not one of the foresters dared to approach it, and gradually the truth was forgotten, as fearsome rumours began to spread about the castle and those who slept within it. Some said that a devilish wizard lived there, brewing potions and chanting his evil spells. Others thought that inside was a mound of treasure guarded by a giant serpent. Many believed that the castle was cursed, and that anyone who entered would be turned to stone.

One fine morning, after the passing of a hundred years, a king's son went hunting in that part of the land. He spied the topmost turrets of the castle through the trees, and asked the foresters about them. Everyone had a different story to tell, and the king's son became utterly confused. But, at last, he came upon an old woodcutter, who said to him: "Many long years ago I was told by my grandfather that inside that castle there lies a beautiful young princess, who is bewitched in some strange way. She has been sleeping for many long years; it is said that only the kiss of a handsome prince will arouse her."

The king's son thanked him heartily and forged ahead, eager to reach the castle. With his sword, he hacked his way through the dense undergrowth, until, at last, he reached the silent castle. As he stood before the castle gates, they swung open for him to enter. Slowly the king's son walked through the long cold passages until he came to the great hall. He stopped still for a moment in amazement. For there, before him, lay the king and queen and all their courtiers, some slumped over the table, some outstretched on the floor. Only by the faint sound of snoring could the prince tell that they were not dead, but merely sleeping.

He made his way past the frozen figures, climbed the broad staircase and walked through several rooms until he reached a large room with a beautiful young girl lying asleep on a bed.

The king's son, moved beyond words by her beauty, bowed down and kissed her hand. After a moment, she opened her eyes, and gazed at him. "Who are you?" she murmured sleepily. "Who is it who has woken me from this deep slumber?" "It is I," answered the prince modestly, "and you, surely, must be the Sleeping Beauty." He was so enchanted that he stayed with her and listened to her story. And then he told her about his coming to the wood and how he had battled his way through dense undergrowth in order to reach her. At last he asked her to marry him.

As the young prince and his princess talked, and made plans to return to his kingdom, the inhabitants of the castle slowly began to stir. The prince led his future bride down the wide staircase and into the great hall with its gilded mirrors. There they were greeted with great joy by the king and queen and by all the courtiers and, before the assembled company, they announced their forthcoming marriage. "We'll hold the wedding this very day!" cried the delighted king and, indeed, that is what they did. The wedding celebrations lasted for many weeks but at last the prince returned home with his Sleeping Beauty, and they lived happily together for many long years.

The Hare and the Tortoise

Once upon a time there lived a hare who
was most terribly vain. One day, when he spotted a
tortoise plodding along the pathway, he could not
resist bounding up to him and boasting:

"Oh, how lucky I am to be a hare! I do so pity you, my friend!"

"Why?" asked the tortoise. "I'm perfectly happy to be a tortoise. Indeed, I pity you! How tiresome to be a hare, dashing hither and thither, never stopping for a single moment to think!"

"Hee hee hee!" retorted the hare. "I simply can't imagine being a plodding tortoise like you! While I am light and gay and graceful, you are slow and dull and heavy. I can run further in a couple of minutes than you can run in a whole day!"

"That's as may be, but why don't you race me and prove it?" challenged the brave tortoise, knowing that he really didn't stand a chance against the swift young hare.

The hare was greatly amused at this offer, but scornfully he agreed to a race. How amusing it would be to humiliate the

wretched tortoise! And so the race was set for the following day, and the fox was appointed to act as judge.

The day of the race dawned bright and clear.

"*Ready . . . Steady . . . GO!*" cried the fox, as soon as the hare and the tortoise were lined up at the starting post. Off bounded the hare, gambolling and skipping along, waving and chattering to friends, stopping to nibble at lettuce leaves and, every now and again, turning around to mock the tortoise.

But the day was a hot and steamy one and the hare soon grew tired. "Why shouldn't I stop for a little nap?" he asked himself. "I can overtake that pathetic tortoise whenever I please." So he lay down by the roadside and dropped off to sleep. Meanwhile, the valiant tortoise plodded along in his usual manner, slow and steady. On and on he lumbered, past the dozing hare and right up to the finishing post. When the hare awoke from a dream about carrots he discovered that the tortoise had won the race and gained the prize. You may be sure that this vain hare never again boasted about his swiftness.

The Gingerbread Man

Once upon a time there lived a little old man and a little old woman who had no children of their own. One day the woman turned to her husband and said: "I think I'll make a tasty gingerbread man for tea." And so she set to work and, before you knew it, there was the gingerbread man with his big shiny currant eyes and his handsome round orange nose and his three smart pink buttons.

The little old woman, pleased as can be, popped him into the oven and trotted off to feed the hens. When she returned to the kitchen, she opened the oven door and carefully removed her gingerbread man. He was done to a turn. "You'll make a tasty mouthful for our tea; we'll have you gobbled up in no time," she said to him, smacking her lips as she spoke.

"Oh, no you won't!" muttered the gingerbread man as she left the room, "nobody is going to gobble me up." And with that he leapt down from the table and was out of the door in a flash.

"Stop! stop!" cried the old woman as the gingerbread man rushed past her at the speed of light. But he, in his piping little voice, called after her:

> *"Run, run as fast as you can,*
> *You can't catch me, I'm the gingerbread man!"*

"Hi there, come back, you can't do that," she

shouted. "Catch him, catch him," she called to the little old man and off they ran down the lane as fast as they could.

As for the gingerbread man, he took not a jot of notice. On and on he raced until he met two children carrying little bundles of firewood. "Stop! stop!" they yelled, brandishing firewood in the air and joining in the chase, "you look delicious!" But the gingerbread man took no heed. And he called out:

"Run, run as fast as you can,
You can't catch me, I'm the gingerbread man!"

And the little old man and the little old woman and the boy and the girl took chase.

Soon the gingerbread man met a cow who blinked at him in surprise. "Stop! stop!" mooed the cow, "you look like a crunchy, munchy boy."

But the gingerbread man took no notice. He just ran faster and faster, and shouted at the top of his voice:

"Run, run as fast as you can,
You can't catch me, I'm the gingerbread man!"

And as he ran he shouted: "I have run away from a little old man and a little old woman, a boy and a girl and I can run away from you too."

And on and on the gingerbread man ran, until he met some haymakers working in a field. They looked up from their work and saw the gingerbread man dashing along by the side of their field.

"Stop! stop!" they shouted, "you can't run along like that, we'd like you for our tea!" But the gingerbread man only laughed and taunted them:

"Run, run as fast as you can,
You can't catch me, I'm the gingerbread man!"

And as he ran on, he called out to them: "I have run away from a little old man and a little old woman, a boy and a girl, and a great big cow and I can certainly run away from you too." And the little old man and the little old woman and the boy and the girl and the cow and the haymakers ran faster and faster but still they could not catch up with the gingerbread man.

On and on the little fellow ran until he came to a field close by a river. "Help, what can I do now," he wailed. "The little old man and the little old woman and the boy and the girl and the cow and the haymakers all want to gobble me up and I cannot cross this river." As he stared at the water, wondering what to do, a fox sidled up to him: "Let me help you," he said, "I can swim over the river with you on my tail. Come on, jump on before it's too late."

And off they went wading across the river. As the water got deeper, the fox called out: "You're getting wet, my dear; move

up closer to my head," and the gingerbread man thanked the fox and jumped right up onto his neck.

And as they crossed a little further the gingerbread man called out: "Please help me, my legs are touching the water," and the fox replied: "In that case you'd better jump right up onto my nose."

So the gingerbread man climbed up onto the tip of the fox's nose and as soon as he did so – *SNAP* – the fox gobbled him up in one great gollop. And now there was no more gingerbread man for the little old man and the little old woman and the boy and the girl and the cow and all the haymakers, and as they stared at the fox on the other side of the river they suddenly felt very hungry.

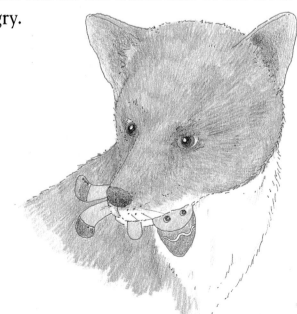

Hans in Luck

Once upon a time there was a hard-working boy called Hans who, for seven long years, worked for a farmer. One day Hans asked the farmer: "Master, I've served you well, now can I leave you to be with my mother." "Of course, of course you can go, Hans, but I must reward you first." That said, the farmer left the room. He returned only moments later, carrying a piece of silver as big as his head. "This is for all the hard work you've done, Hans," said the farmer as he presented him with the silver ball.

Hans was delighted. Without delay he pulled a square of cloth out of his pocket, wrapped up the silver ball, heaved it over his shoulder and set off on his travels.

Before he had gone a few miles Hans started to feel tired and hot. He was shuffling slowly along, dragging one foot after the other, when he saw a horseman trotting towards him. "Ah!" cried Hans, "what a lucky man! No tripping against stones, no wearing out his shoes; in fact he doesn't have to make any effort at all." The horseman stopped and chuckled: "Well, my boy, what makes you so tired, then?" Hans pointed to the big round lump on his back: "That's the trouble! It's silver, so heavy you wouldn't believe it. I can't even hold my head up properly." "No problem," said the horseman, "we'll swop. You give me the silver, I give you the horse." "Wonderful, wonderful," exclaimed Hans, "but I warn you, you'll certainly get tired dragging that lump around with you." The horseman only smiled and, leaping from his animal, grabbed the silver and handed the bridle to Hans. "Now then, listen to me: when you want the horse to go fast, well, just smack your lips hard and shout out 'Jip'."

Hans was thrilled and sitting bolt upright on the horse, he rode merrily on his way. Soon he decided to go faster. He smacked his lips and cried "Jip" at the top of his voice. Off charged the horse and before Hans could draw breath, there he was lying in a ditch by the roadside. His horse went charging off but a butcher, wheeling a pig in a barrow, grabbed hold of the bridle. Then he led the horse back to Hans and watched as the lad dusted himself down and staggered to his feet.

"This riding is no joke," Hans muttered, "after all how would you feel if you rode a beast like this? I'm not riding that creature again. Tell you the truth, I like your pig a great deal better." "Well," said the butcher, "easily sorted out. I'll take your horse, you take

my pig." No sooner had Hans nodded his agreement than the butcher leapt onto the horse, and away he rode.

As Hans jogged along, the pig trotting by his side, he couldn't help thinking what a lucky fellow he was. And when a countryman, carrying a fine white goose under his arm, stopped to greet him, Hans told him all about his luck. The countryman listened, then showed Hans the goose: "Feel how heavy it is, and only eight weeks old. Whoever roasts and eats this creature is a lucky man!" "You're right," said Hans prodding the goose, "but my pig's heavy, too." "Ah," said the countryman, "but your pig spells trouble. In that village over there, the farmer's pig has disappeared. Don't get caught or they'll hurl you right into the horse-pond."

Poor Hans was badly frightened. "Good man," he cried, "please take my pig and give me the goose in return." "Well, just as a favour then," agreed the man as he handed over the goose.

Now, as Hans came to the last village on his journey, a knife-grinder came up to him: "What a splendid goose! How much did it cost you?" "Oh I didn't buy it," Hans explained, "I exchanged it for a pig." "And where did you get the pig?" said the man. "I gave a horse for it." "And the horse?" "I

gave silver for it and, oh, I worked hard for the money for seven long years." "Now if you turn grinder like me," said the man, "you'll have money for the rest of your life. Here, give me the goose, I'll hand you the stone."

But soon Hans found the heavy stone weighing him down and he dropped it at the edge of a pond while he stooped down for a drink. And as he bent over he nudged the stone plunging it straight into the water. Hans watched as it sank deeper and deeper, then up he sprang: "How happy am I," he cried "to be rid of that heavy stone. No one was ever so lucky as I am." And free of all troubles Hans ran home to his mother.

The Eagle and the Rabbits

One fine day in the midst of summer, when the wheat was golden and the oats still green, a rabbit was sitting in the grass with her two young children. All of a sudden an eagle swooped down, seized the children in her talons, and carried them aloft.

The horrified rabbit raced after the eagle, imploring her to spare her two little ones. But the wicked eagle had no pity in her heart: "Go away, or I'll eat you up too!" she cried. "My children are hungry and your children will make a tasty meal for them."

In sorrow and anger, the mother rabbit returned home and summoned a meeting. When all the rabbits were gathered together, she begged them to help her punish the eagle. "Ah, but none of us could ever harm a great,

all-powerful eagle,"
muttered one grumpy old
rabbit, "leave well alone, and
just be thankful that you're
alive." "But surely we could
defeat the ruthless bird if only all of
us worked together!" pleaded the mother
rabbit.

And that is exactly what they did. Day
after day, the rabbits stood around the tree
in which the eagle lived, and gnawed
and gnawed and gnawed at its roots.

The eagle was too busy feeding her young to notice anything. At last, the rabbits broke through the hard roots and, with a great crash, the tree toppled over. All the little eaglets were shaken from their nest and fell to the ground. Waiting for them at the foot of the tree was a big hungry fox. Without a second's hesitation, he opened his mouth wide and gobbled them all up. And the heartless eagle never again in her life bothered the rabbits.